Pirates of the Seven Seas

Book One: Gromund's Tales
Ravi Struck & Josh Weisman

PIRATES OF THE SEVEN SEAS
Book One: Gromund's Tales
Copyright © 2018, Ravi Struck & Josh Weisman

ISBN (Print Edition): 978-1-54392-226-4
ISBN (eBook Edition): 978-1-54392-227-1

Pirates
of the
Seven Seas

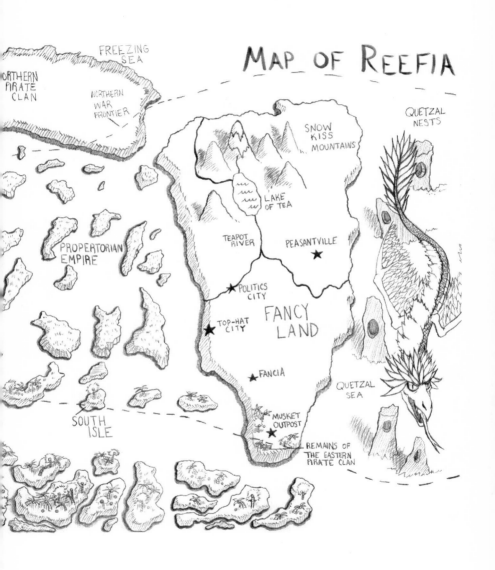

MAP OF REEFIA

FREEZING
SEA

NORTHERN
PIRATE
CLAN

NORTHERN
WAR
FRONTIER

QUETZAL
NESTS

SNOW
KISS
MOUNTAINS

LAKE
OF TEA

PROPERTORIAN
EMPIRE

TEAPOT
RIVER

PEASANTVILLE ★

★ POLITICS
CITY

FANCY
LAND

★ TOP-HAT
CITY

QUETZAL
SEA

★ FANCIA

SOUTH
ISLE

★ MUSKET
OUTPOST

REMAINS OF
THE EASTERN
PIRATE CLAN

Table Of Contents

Prologue

'Ello, Friends. I'm Gromund, and I've been a pirate for 50 years. My job is to take supplies from Skull Island and transfer it to Cutlass's crew (you'll learn about him later). Now, I've got a story to tell. It all began in the summer. Two pirate clans—the Western Pirate Clan and Southern Pirate Clan—raided South Isle, which is part of the Propertorian Empire (simply called "Propers" by pirates). It was the largest and most powerful empire in Reefia, not to mention the fanciest. It was made up of a mainland, called Fancy Land, South Isle and many other smaller islands. South Isle had a beautiful landscape with a massive sea wall protecting it, but was only one mile wide, making it a rather small island. The Western Pirates and Southern Pirates began their attack at 4 o'clock in the morning when only night scouts were still awake.

At the Sea Wall

"General, pirates are approaching from the West," reported a scout on the seawall.

"All men to arms, load the cannons, ring the bell, get troops to the shore. There's no time to waste," commanded the general looking through a telescope. His eyes widened when he saw the flag. It had a skull with a big sword in the center of it. "Blackblade!" The general whispered to himself.

Blackblade was an evil, imposing figure with black hair, average-length black beard, and a big black sword he carried always. Blackblade oversaw a clan of pirates known to most as the Western Pirate Clan.

With fear in his eyes, the general shouted orders to his men. "Double the troops and send in the ships. We need more soldiers. All men on deck!"

Then, the general boarded a navy ship and headed off to fight the pirates. Sadly, the ship was hit by cannons once in firing range of Blackblade's crew and sank within minutes. The general soon drown.

While all this was happening, no one noticed the other pirate ship coming from the South. Its flag was a skull with two cutlasses forming an "x". It was the ship of Captain Cutlass.

The two ships made landfall on different sides of South Isle. Blackblade landed West, Cutlass landed South.

It was no longer than five to ten minutes before the only town of South Isle was in flames. The Western Pirate Clan came charging in, setting fire to everything in sight, slaughtering and butchering people, and laughing all the while. Dead bodies littered the muddy streets. Screams and cries were heard everywhere. At the same time, the Southern Pirates, unnoticed by anyone, were stealing gold and silver, but barely killed a soul.

The Duel

In the middle of all this, there was a boy named Rick. He was only four with brown hair and tannish skin. He was crying on the cold, muddy ground next to his house on the South Isle shore. His mother had been shot dead in the attack. His father was the Supreme Admiral of the Proper Navy, meaning he was busy battling pirates. Around Rick's neck was a golden medallion.

Soon after Rick began crying, Blackblade showed up next to him. He reached for the medallion. Yet, in the blink of an eye, a blade came down right in front of his hand. It was Cutlass's blade.

"Ah Cutlass, what brings you here. Loot, bounties, or maybe, I don't know, me?"

"Loot and the boy," Cutlass replied.

"Oh no, the lad is as good as dead. Now back off or I will kill ya' and the lad."

"Do you even know who he is?"

"Of course, I do. He's a worthless boy with a valuable medallion that's mine for the taking!"

"No, he's our great nephew, ye know, Romeo's son."

"Too bad," Blackblade said dismissively. Then he quickly pushed Cutlass's blade out of his way and tried to grab the medallion. But before he could touch it, Cutlass slashed the side of his left hand.

"Argh! Ye stupid sea rat. I'll kill ye!"

Before Blackblade could even take out his sword, Cutlass jabbed him again, this time in the right hip. To Cutlass's surprise, Blackblade didn't seem to feel pain despite the bleeding. He just said, "ouch" and pulled the blade right out of his hip. Cutlass drew his second cutlass, all the while puzzled that Blackblade wasn't slowed by his injuries.

"Ha, serves you right for trying to kill family," Cutlass snarled. His voice was now full of rage. He cared about family a lot.

"Raugh, I hate you," Blackblade screamed, drawing his sword, the Ebony Blade.

The two got into a ferocious duel. Clang cling, clang, cling, clang, clang, cling, went the blades. Occasionally, they would shoot their pistols, narrowly missing each other. Soon, Blackblade and Cutlass were drenched in blood from head to toe. Their limbs trembled. They both were severely injured.

Cutlass was on the floor and Blackblade was about to land the final death blow when suddenly he heard, "**CANNONBALL!**" Brunt (the ship's brute) and Timmy (the ship's four-foot-tall Spaniard) yelled as a cannon shot a humongous cannonball right at the house. **BOOM!** The house burst into flames.

"Capitano," Timmy said in his heavy Spanish accent, "we must get out of here!"

"Right! Bring the boy, we need him," Cutlass commanded.

"Yes, Captain." Brunt said, who, with Timmy's help, had rowed a dinghy to pick them up. Brunt picked up Rick, Timmy helped up Cutlass and together they fled the burning house, leaving Blackblade in the rubble.

Leaving in Ruins

A lieutenant reported to Rick's father Romeo that the Western and Southern Pirate ships had left, as did the Proper's ships, leaving the town in ruins.

"Admiral," the lieutenant asked, "should we pursue?"

"No. This defeat was a minor setback. Not enough to topple the great Propertorian Empire. We will expand

North, South and West and we will eliminate these pirate clans," Romeo said. With that, he turned the ship around and sailed to Fancy Land, the Propertorian mainland.

A few hours later, a soldier reported to Romeo that his wife had been shot dead on South Isle and his son was missing. Romeo was devastated. Overcome with grief, he wept in front of the messenger. For the following six months, he was in a deep depression.

Chapter 1:
14 Years Later

I, Gromund was promoted to weapons' inspector and repairman of a ship called the Plunderer. This meant my job was to tell Cutlass the state of our guns and swords, and repair anything broken on the ship. Anyway, enough about me. This story is about Rick and the adventures he had in this world called Reefia.

On Deck

Rick was one of Captain Cutlass's fishers. Occasionally he was called on board the main ship, the Plunderer, to swab the decks. **Splat!** Was what Rick heard as he dropped the mop to check his work. The deck looked spotless to Rick, but Captain Cutlass said, "you missed a spot over there, lady."

Cutlass was the leader of the Southern Pirate Clan. He was six feet tall, stronger than an average pirate, with white hair and a short white beard, who wore a green jacket with gold buttons outlined in black. All around

Reefia, he was known as a fierce fighter.

Cutlass and his crew had raised Rick ever since he was a boy. But none of them seemed to treat him with any respect. None, that is, except for Chief Fisher Morano and Nettle the Nurse. They thought Rick was something special.

"When you're done swabbing the deck, you nuisance," Cutlass yelled, "return to the Grouper for a fishing session. We've been low on fish for the past three weeks."

When Rick returned to the Grouper, their fishing boat, he was happy to see Morano. He had a black goatee and long black hair, and wore a light green shirt and blue pants with a straw hat.

"I just don't understand," he told Morano, "they keep me on the Plunderer, yet treat me like fish guts."

"They love ye more than ye think. Cutlass loves ye more than even me. He's puttin' on an act so he won't be mutinied." Morano assured him.

"Why would they treat me so poorly if they care so much?" Rick said confused.

"I can't say. The captain forbids it. He doesn't want ye knowin' about yer past just yet." Morano confided in a soft voice.

"What is he hiding from me?"

"I told ye. I can't say."

Suddenly, **BANG!**

A Mysterious Attack

Bang, Bang, Bang. The shots of a cannon could be heard close by.

"Rick! Quickly, cut the lines! There's an enemy ship approaching from the West. Let's get out of here!" Morano urged, sounding scared.

Morano and Rick rowed hard back to the Plunderer to tell Captain Cutlass about the enemy ship. Cutlass came on deck and took out his spyglass.

"Strange," exclaimed Cutlass, "that ship is flying Blackblade's insignia on its flag, but I thought he died 14 years ago!"

"I thought so too," Morano replied. "Perhaps the Western Pirates have a new leader?" Morano wondered out loud.

"I highly doubt it," Cutlass said quietly, as if to himself. "Only a pirate as strong as Blackblade could unify the Western Pirate Clan. And there are no such pirates in that clan."

After pausing for 30 seconds deep in thought about what to do, Cutlass yelled "Fire," as he realized an enemy ship had advanced right next to the Plunderer.

Cannons launched cannonballs everywhere. While some of Cutlass's pirates lit the gunpowder of the cannons, others started attacking the enemy ship's crew. The enemy ship sunk quickly.

"Why did the ship have Blackblade's insignia on it?" worried Morano.

"Don't know," Cutlass replied, "but we're gonna to find out. Set course for Anthony's Outpost. Time to meet up with an old friend."

Chapter 2:
Yo-Ho-Ho and A Bottle of Rum

The Tavern

Antony's Outpost was once a base of operations used by Propertorian soldiers for their war on the Western and Southern Pirate Clans. It was located southwest of the Sea of Skulls. After years of fighting, the Southern Pirate Clan overtook the Outpost, making it a haven for their pirates. No Proper ships or soldiers had traveled here since.

Rick, Morano, Timmy, Mahanti, the ship's voodoo master, Cutlass and his first mate Tugger headed for a tavern on the Outpost. Upon entering the tavern, Cutlass introduced the crew to his friend and bartender, Goon.

"Hola Goon," Timmy said, "Capitano says you are a good storyteller."

"Indeed," said Goon. "Now Cutlass, what brings ye this far South?"

"Blackblade," Cutlass replied. "I saw his insignia on a ship yesterday and I was wondering how that was possible."

"Ah, a good question, and to answer it, let me tell ye a tale," Goon replied excitedly.

The Tale

"Once upon a time," Goon began, "five years ago, to be exact. Me and my crew were sailing our vessel, the Tiny Bucket, into the Sea of Skulls when we happened upon a massive ship with pitch black wood and rows of cannons. We heard shouts of "yo ho, ho" and at once knew from the insignia it was Blackblade's lead ship, the Dark Serpent. Now, this was just five months before the battle of Skarmada. The pirates could be heard shouting "this will be the most successful battle in Western Pirate history." Then, I heard a brute say, "all hail the captain." I expected to see Blackblade's first mate, but instead a one-legged Blackblade stepped out. He was deep in conversation bragging to his crew about how he survived the siege of South Isle. Apparently, a brute carried him out. His leg had gotten stuck under some rubble, so the brute cut it off. Blackblade tied a stick onto his stump so that he could walk, then the two went to the dock but the Dark Serpent had already left. They stayed on the island for three days feeding on whatever scraps they could find in the ruined town before a merchant ship carried them back to the Western Pirate Clan. Before I could hear the rest of the story, someone from the Dark Serpent suddenly yelled "intruder" and I quickly realized we had been spotted. Cannonballs came flying at us. I was the only one to escape, thanks to the dinghy tied to Tiny Bucket."

"There's another thing," Goon said. "Blackblade holds the Ebony Blade. It's made from dark stone and cursed metal. Whoever bears the sword has unbelievable power and strength, including their crew, but there's a down side. If the wielder is killed, he and his clan disappear from the face of Reefia."

Goon ended the story with a ghastly stare. He laughed at the look on Cutlass's, Rick's and the rest of the crew's face and said, "well what are ye sittin' there for." He lifted his glass and said, "Yo ho, ho and a bottle of rum."

In response everyone in the tavern repeated and drank their rum except for Rick who was enjoying a traditional pirate drink which was made from squeezed Licheeberries. Licheeberries were small fruits around 4 inches in diameter. The fruit was white and grew only on Coconut Island in the Mango Sea. Coconut Island was also known as fruit paradise since many of the fruits in Reefia grew there.

The Dog

At around 10 o'clock at night, Cutlass and his crew left the tavern drunk and tired, and headed back to the Plunderer. Most of the crew was already asleep when they arrived. Everyone went inside to sleep except Rick. He noticed a lit candle dangerously close to one of the sails. He quickly put out the candle, and turned to go inside when he noticed Dunchest, the ship's dog (a Proper Mastiff) was still on deck looking in different directions. You see Dunchest is a watchdog. He doesn't need to keep watch when they're totally safe like tonight, but he just can't help himself, it's his duty.

"C'mon Duny," Rick said, "there's nothing to be afraid of, we're safe." But Dunchest didn't move, not a bit.

"C'mon you wanna treat?" Rick took a biscuit from his pocket, but before he could say another word, Dunchest was inside sitting and waiting for his treat. After getting his biscuit, he barked thanks and went to sleep on his pillow. Rick then went to sleep soundly in his hammock.

Chapter 3:
Treasure and The Truth

The Questions

Rick had lots of questions. Why was the medallion around his neck when he was a kid so special? Why did Cutlass and the crew treat him so badly (except Morano and Nettle)? And most of all, who were his mother and father?

He went to Chief Fisher Morano's chamber to ask these questions. He got this reply:

"I'm not supposed to tell ye, but 100 years ago, a pirate with magical powers named Avatorios used his powers to locate the island with the portal to Oceanus, a mysterious world full of mystics. Now, this island is very difficult to find because it's not on maps. It's called the Isle of the Avatorios Seas. Avatorios hid his treasure there knowing that bandits, robbers, and pirates who were after the loot would never find it. Once his treasure was hidden, Avatorios then sunk the Isle to the bottom of Avatorios Sea using his magical powers. In the same spot, he created a marble ring with seven slots, one for each medallion. The ring became known as the Circle of Justice. Whoever found all the medallions and placed them in the Circle of Justice would cause the Isle of Avatorios Sea to rise out of the water, gaining access to the treasure and the portal to Oceanus. Avatorios did not want anyone finding his treasure, so he hid the medallions with seven monsters across the Seas of Reefia. Your medallion was hidden with a flying snake that had wide wings called a Quetzal. Quetzals live in island-like nests in the Quetzal Sea to the East of Fancy Land. Anyway, soon people got word of the Isle of the Avatorios Sea. Many tried to get the medallions, but they all died, except the people who got your medallion, the one you had around your neck when Cutlass found you. Eventually, people were too scared to fight the monsters and gave up looking for the medallions. That's all I'm going to say, otherwise I'll be walkin' the plank to Shark Alley." Morano abruptly ended his story, concerned he had given away far too much already.

Sailing for Disaster

The water had something in it, something big and orange with pincers. There was only one word to describe it: **CRABS!**

"Set the sails boys!" Captain Cutlass commanded.

"Where to captain?" Fin asked.

"Follow those crabs," Cutlass replied. "They'll bring use to King Claw Island where we will find the next closest medallion."

"Follow the crabs ye 'orrible lot!" Fin shouted at the crew unaware that in the distance the Dark Serpent had been following the Plunderer.

"It appears Cutlass is also trying to find the medallions. Lads, let's send 'em a message. **FIRE!**" Blackblade ordered.

One after another, the cannonballs barely missed the Plunderer, though one managed to tear a hole on the right side. The crew, caught by surprise, did not know where the blasts were coming from.

"Capin'," said Tugger, "who's shootin' at us?"

"Blackblade!" Cutlass angrily responded as he looked though his telescope. "Fire at that speck over there and let's hurry away."

"But sir they--"

"If they can shoot this far we can too."

Cannons fired cannonballs, but they only went a short way before plummeting into the water. **BANG!** Another enemy cannonball landed on the Plunderer, destroying its largest cannon. There was constant Bang, Bang, Bang, Bang! Cannonballs from the enemy ship continued to bombard the Plunderer.

"Sail away as fast as ye can!" Cutlass yelled to the crew.

The ruined Plunderer raised its sails picking up speed as it followed the crabs away from the Dark Serpent.

Chapter 4:
Crab Click

Wrecked

"Aw, fish cobbler," cursed Cutlass when he looked at his wrecked ship. He turned to Gromund and angrily said, "This is all your fault Gromund. You assured me the Plunderer's cannons could shoot far enough. Instead, our ship is wrecked, our cannons destroyed and you're still standing here, useless. You're fired! Take a dinghy and leave."

I did what I was told, got a dinghy and rowed away as fast as I could, not knowing when I would see my mates again.

Ugh, that wasn't the smartest decision, thought Cutlass. *With Gromund gone, there's no way to fix the Plunderer.*

"Capitano, maybe you should sit this one out." Timmy said. "Because of your uncontrollable temper, we lost our best repairman. Now we have no way to get home or defend ourselves. Blackblade can ambush us and all we have are swords, pistols and a few working cannons." Timmy sighed, wishing Gromund was still there.

"Let's just find the next medallion instead of complaining. Even in a wrecked ship, we managed to reach King Claw Island." Cutlass snapped defiantly.

To change the subject, Rick asked Cutlass if he wanted to use his prized bronze pistol for the upcoming fight.

"You mean that rusty, old non-functioning excuse for a pistol? I'd rather use my gold laced pistol. It never misses a shot." Cutlass replied.

"That is just rude. Me and the crew spent all our gold coins buying a rare bronze pistol at an antique shop in Mango City for your birthday last year. The shop owner said it was in pristine condition, only been used one time about a century ago. All this time you've never cared for our precious gift. You've been lying to us pretending to like it! Capitano, you taught us lying is an offense. Now you have committed an offense. I say we make you pay by fighting the great crustacean king to get the medallion. Who's with me?" Timmy asked, hoping his speech persuaded the crew to punish Cutlass.

All the pirates, including Rick yelled, "Yaaarrrrrrrr!!" Then the crew docked the boat in the gulf of King Claw Island, pushed Cutlass off the boat and escorted him to the center of the island to fight the crustacean king, known as King Claw, for the medallion.

Dunchest was howling when he saw Cutlass heading to the King Claw. Dunchest hated when Cutlass left him alone. He was always scared that he wouldn't return.

"Aaroo, Aaroo," howled Dunchest until he was out of breath and then he began to whimper realizing Cutlass was not coming back until the mission was over.

King Claw

In the center of King Claw Island there was an army of big crabs around seven feet wide five feet in length, and the bigger ones were eight feet wide and six feet in length. The crabs they had followed exited the water with food to hand out. The crabs feasted angrily on fish and seaweed. Then the biggest of the crabs went to the center and gave a shark to....

"Wait, am I seeing right? The ruler of all these crabs is a **TITANIC LOBSTER**!!! Why a lobster, not a crab? That's practically asking a different species to be your king." Rick blurted out in confusion.

The lobster was darkish red with huge pincers, and antennas as long as a mast of a ship. The scariest part was his enormous fan-like tail. When his tail moved, it made a strong gust of wind that caused the crabs behind him to go flying into the air.

"Greetings piratesss," King Claw, the giant lobster said, as his pincers went click, click, click. "Who is yer leader?"

Timmy pushed Cutlass forward.

"I am Captain Cutlass. Leader of the Southern Pirate Clan."

"Ooohhh, what an opportunity," King Claw said, taking a bite out of a dead shark. "That means I will eee-aaattt youuuu laaassst. **Crabs put them on the stove**."

Crabs came crawling down from the mountain and tried to put them on the stove but then Rick did something foolish. He saw the battle arena and shouted, "I challenge you to a duel!"

"Yyyyyou chchchchallenge meee?" King Claw replied amused. "Very weelll. Choose yoourrrr weapon. Ttthhee baaattlllleee will cooommmmense at 7 o'clock in the morning."

King Claw pulled out a musket, a pistol and a harpoon. Rick chose the harpoon.

"Noooo!" Cutlass yelled, "You should have chosen the musket!"

"Trust me, I have a plan." Rick replied and went to his chamber for the night.

The Duel

Early the next morning Rick entered the battlefield with his harpoon. There were crabs everywhere cheering and screaming nonsensical chants in a language he didn't understand. In the middle of the commotion stood his crew, watching, waiting. They knew after Rick faced his doom, they would face theirs. King Claw jumped to the center of the ring, his pincers clicking, his face ready. Rick held the harpoon in starting position. The umpire started the countdown. The spectators followed along. "**3, 2, 1, FIGHT!**"

The fight began. Rick ran along the curved walls. King Claw ran to the wall snapping at him. He was faster than Rick had imagined so he would have to change his strategy. King Claw snipped at Rick, ripping his pants. Rick tried to use astonishing speed but King Claw cornered him against the wall.

"Ttttimmee to eat." King Claw said gleefully.

"King Claw, you're getting too fat from eating pirates."

"Wrrrroonng, fooollll!"

King Claw snipped at Rick with his other pincer but he missed. Rick yelled, "Hey King Claw, time for your drop off." Rick yanked his harpoon and threw it at King Claw's head.

"Aaaaaaahhhhhhhhhhhhhh!" King Claw yelled as the harpoon struck him. He tried pulling the harpoon out, but it just made things worse. King Claw wasn't finished yet. He lunged his claw at Rick, but in the nick of time Rick leaped towards King Claw. He grabbed hold of the harpoon still in King Claw's head and with all his might pushed the harpoon deeper in to King Claw.

"Ahhhhhhhhhhhhhhhhhhhhhhhhhhhhhhhhhhh!" King Claw screamed as he plummeted into the arena, dead. All the crabs bowed their heads at Rick.

"What is it you command, master?" Said one of the crabs in the stands. Killing King Claw apparently made Rick their new leader.

"Wait, crabs are good builders, right?"

"True." The crab replied.

"Then follow me. I've got something to fix."

"**Fixy, fixy, fixy, fixy, fixy, fixy**." Said all the crabs. They went to the beach and used their bodies to fill in the holes of the Plunderer. Rick suddenly remembered what they were here for: **the medallion**.

"Tugger go get the ship ready for departure, I just need to tinkle in the bushes."

Rick headed to the bushes and came out the other side. He saw a big temple-like structure which he thought held the medallion. He ran up behind it and went through a back door. Inside was a big gold column, on top was the medallion, but there were around 10 to 20 crab guards surrounding it. Rick had a plan. He tossed a coin in the air. It landed in between two guards.

"Ooohh a coin, it's mine!" One of the guards gleefully said.

"No, it landed on my side!" Another crab said. The two got into a fight until one guard knocked the other over, who knocked the other over and so on. Soon, all the guards where fighting. Rick easily walked in and removed the medallion from the column. Little did he know, the column was an alarm of sorts. When Rick removed the medallion, the weight lessened on the column triggering a loud gong to ring which made all the guards look up to see Rick holding medallion.

"Get him, he's stealing the medallion!"

Soon enough, Rick was chased by all the crab guards in the temple. He ran into a hallway leading to a room full of weapons. Rick grabbed a sword and a musket. He then ran back into the hallway and out of the temple. He ran so fast his shoes began to hurt his feet.

The Battle

He turned around on the beach to see the crabs had made a line in which they held muskets specially made for their claws. A crab in the center raised both his claws up in the air in surrender. The crabs in the line looked at what he was looking at, and sure enough there was the Plunderer with at least five cannons about to fire.

"Make 'em into crab stew boys, **fire!**" Cutlass yelled. Cannonballs flew from the Plunderer directly towards the crabs. **BOOM BOOM BOOM**. The crabs went flying.

"Moldy fish guts! We just lost half of our defenses." A crab general said, arriving at the battlefield with more troops. They arranged themselves in another line.

"Aim. Fire!" Bullets went flying everywhere. Rick ducked in time not to get hit. He then shot a crab with his musket. Bam! The crab fell down dead. Then he shot again, bam and again, bam. Soon there were only six crabs left, but these ones were very, very big ones, though slow; and worse, they were manning cannons aimed at the Plunderer. Rick shot one, but its shell was too thick. Rick needed something long to stick under the shell to kill them. A harpoon, he thought, and ran to the Plunderer. He saw the Grouper tied to the back of the ship. He quickly ran into the shallow warm water to get to the back of the boat and then went into the Grouper and took a harpoon off the rack. He ran back and behind the giant crabs, stabbing one of them right between where the top and bottom plate shells meet.

"Eeep!" The crab said, falling to the ground and squirting blood all over Rick.

"Ewww!" Rick said. He then went to another crab from behind. This time the crab next to it pinched Rick's leg and made a big cut. Rick yelled in pain as he fell to the floor.

Back at the Plunderer the crew was about to go help Rick but around 100 crabs climbed onto the ship including the ones filling in the holes.

"Attack!" Yelled Cutlass. They were forced to attack the crabs instead of helping Rick. He could see Mahanti throwing sleep dust at crabs and Timmy firing pistols at a crab.

One of the crabs was about to stab Rick with a knife when Rick stabbed it in the pincer and then weaved his harpoon through the plate of the crab.

"EEEEEEEE!" The crab was in so much pain, it lost too much blood and died. Rick only had a few more crabs left and they were advancing faster than the earlier crabs. Every step he made he lost more blood from his leg and it was ever so painful. He could only sit and wait for the right time to strike. One crab now had a musket and was aiming for Rick's head. Rick only had one choice, run! He ran with great speed, but his wound kept squirting blood making him slower by the minute.

"Help! Somebody help! Cutlass, Morano, help!" No one answered. Only a crab laughing about the tragedy he was about to face. But Rick wasn't done. He still had the medallion in his hand and he had a good three minutes until the slow crabs would catch up. It wasn't long until Rick found a gunpowder storage room. He took a match out of his pocket and lit it, then dropped it in a barrel of gunpowder. He then ran so fast out of the storage room that his leg was entirely drenched in blood. **KABOOM**!!! All the crabs went flying in the air, landing with a thud and splashing blood all over Rick-- **splat**. He fell to the ground clenching his leg. He looked up to see crabs fleeing from the Plunderer and into the jungle of King Claw Island. Rick was still clutching the medallion when he saw the Plunderer's crew running towards him. He held it up high so everyone could see. Suddenly, everything went black. He had fainted from blood loss.

Chapter 5:

Truth or Trust

Conversations with Cutlass

Rick woke up in the ship's infirmary, his body covered in bandages. Nettle the Nurse was sitting next to him treating a wound on his arm.

"Ah awake, finally! Cutlass was worried thinking you were dead. I'll go tell him you're awake. Stay put, you're weaker than you think." Nettle quickly left the room to go find Cutlass.

Rick was surprised to hear Cutlass was worried about him. That's something he thought he would never hear, but somehow it was all starting to make sense. Morano was right, Cutlass did care about him. Like yesterday's battle with the crabs and Crustacean King. Cutlass was the one who told the crew to fire at the crabs as they were about to kill Rick. Rick felt happy, a weird happy, but

29

happy nonetheless. Just then, Cutlass walked in the room, closing the door behind him so it was only him and Rick.

"When I saw what you did with those crabs, I knew you were going to be captain of the Plunderer someday." Cutlass said smiling proudly, something he didn't do often.

Rick felt confused. He didn't understand. How could a fisherman end up a captain? Besides, he was only eighteen years old. It would be at least another twenty years before he qualified to be captain.

Cutlass seemed to read his mind. "We're pirates," he said. "We don't follow the rules."

"Then why are rules made in the first place?" Rick asked.

"Because some stupid people, like the privateers of the East follow them, but we Southern Pirates live to break rules and make our own rules."

Having Cutlass by his side made Rick felt better. And hearing Cutlass say he was going to be captain of his own ship someday eased Rick's nerves and made him feel confident.

Meanwhile at the Western Pirate Clan

"You lost the medallion to a kid?" Blackblade yelled in dismay at his general.

"Well this kid came running towards us with dozens of crabs after him and---"

"Ye could have just killed the crabs and the kid and go with the medallion." Why didn't you?" Blackblade asked bewildered.

"Well, we were scared," said the general.

"What!! You were scared? You must pay for this failure!" Blackblade shouted in anger.

"But I'm broke," said the general.

"Then say hello to the toddler." Blackblade pulled out Ebony Blade and killed the general. He then ordered his men to find Cutlass and retrieve the medallion.

The Family Tree

The next day Rick felt a bit stronger than the day before. Rick knew that Cutlass was hiding something. Something big, something surprising. He thought it had to do with his blood line. Why did he think this? He had a feeling that the medallion on his neck wasn't the only reason Cutlass took care of him since he was boy. Now that he knew Cutlass cared for him, Rick wanted to see the family tree. It was something extremely special. If you were caught looking at the family tree you would be killed or you would have to walk the plank! Rick wanted to see it more than ever now. He wanted the truth now that he had Cutlass's trust, but he worried. What if he lost his trust? What if he became worthless again? Rick thought about how he had gotten the medallion by defeating around 40 crabs by himself, and by that Rick knew he had the trust of Cutlass.

"Nettle?" Rick called.

"Yes dear, what is it? More pain?"

"No, I want to see Cutlass again."

"Oh, of course dear. I'll go get him." Nettle left and in about a minute Cutlass was there in front of him, a grin on his face.

"Cutlass, I hope it's not too much to ask but---."

"Ye wanna see the family tree, don't ya? I know, it's in me pocket." Cutlass pulled out a piece of parchment paper, unrolling it carefully to reveal the heading at the top of the paper: **Avatorios Family Tree**.

The family tree was not as big as others. Some distant family members were excluded but it had the main parts. At last, Rick saw his origins. His jaw dropped. His bloodline went all the way to the Great Avatorios who ruled the Seven Seas for 70 years and was said to have magical powers. The one who created all seven medallions and hid them across Reefia. His jaw dropped even further when he saw Blackblade and Cutlass were brothers! This meant Cutlass and Blackblade were his Great Uncles! He also realized that Cutlass had another brother Dorth who married Tulo and gave birth to Romeo, his father! He was also part of the family! Rick noticed there were skulls near some of the names.

"Why are there skulls near these names," Rick asked.

"Death," Cutlass said frowning. "Avatorios died of old age same with Almea, but Gothus, John, Dorth and Tulo, and how can I forget, your mother Martha died at the hands of Blackblade. They had information about where some of the medallions were located, but they refused to tell Blackblade, so he killed them."

Rick's face went pale. Blackblade had killed a good fourth of his family. This was shocking and hard for Rick to make sense of.

"Wait, how is Nettle still alive? She was born around the same time as Avatorios."

"Well ye see Nettle is special. She ate magical Turgoberries. These berries extend your life for 100 to 200 more years." Cutlass stared at the door where Nettle was waiting behind.

"Lad, now you've seen the tree and heard about your family. Best get some rest. I gotta go see if we're headin' on the right course. Wheeler is steering the ship but he's a little dizzy and is losing his sense of direction." On that note Cutlass left to go steer the ship to their next destination.

Chapter 6:
Boom Bang Boom

On the Decks

The Plunderer creaked every time a wave came rolling in. Having fired Gromund, Cutlass was desperate for a builder and tools to fix the ship.

"Argh, we are headin' North. We're supposed to be heading South. Wheeler, yer head isn't working right. I'm commanding ye to go to Nettle," Cutlass said. Wheeler walked zig zagging through the door to the infirmary.

"Boys we need more wind in the sails or we'll never get the Plunderer to Buildaroo Island for repairs." Cutlass lamented.

He chose Buildaroo Island because it had the closest repair shop that allowed pirate ships. But first they had to get the damaged Plunderer there. The crew was running from one end of the ship to the next with new sails to put up and tattered ones to pull down. Some were lifting sails higher to catch more wind, others putting ores in the water and rowing, and still more crewmates were throwing useless stuff over board to make the ship lighter.

The Enemy

Rick looked through the circle window next to his bed in the infirmary. There was something in the distance. Rick squinted hard and saw a ship with a flag, the flag of the Western Pirate Clan.

"Nettle, Nettle, Nettle!" Rick cried.

"What is it dear? Did a wound open up?"

"No, worse, Blackblade! See the ship in the distance, it has Blackblade's insignia!"

"Oh dear! I must tell Cutlass right away. Stay put, you're in no shape for fighting. Wheeler, you stay put too, you've got a fever." Nettle then ran out of the infirmary. Soon enough Rick could hear the shouts and complaints of the crew fighting over what to do.

He heard Cutlass say, "Move faster they'll never catch up."

Then he heard a pirate say, "We are about to sink. The ship's got too many holes." Just then someone else shouted, "There's Buildaroo Island, we're saved!"

Soon enough, through the window, Rick saw land.

Buildaroo Island

From what Rick could see, Buildaroo Island was quite small with just a few trees and one large house. Chains, hooks and all sorts of gizmos hung from every window. The house had a blue roof, grayish wooden siding and a pulley system to bring ships into the yard for repairs. A man around 70 years old with a white goatee, dark wrinkly skin wearing blue overalls with a black shirt walked out of the house down a stone path to the dock.

"Arnold, we need a fix at once. The Plunderer has too many holes and if we end up sinking in Shark Alley, we'll be chomped for sure." Cutlass begged.

"Ye want me to fix yer whole ship in less than a day? Well then, it's gonna cost ya. Let's say 1,500,000 gold debloons plus 2,100,000 Proper coins for taxes and fees. I pay the Propers to live and work on this island. If I don't pay me taxes, the Imperial Fourth Navy's gonna blow my shop to bits."

"We can't afford such a price, plus we don't keep Proper money." Said Rick who had managed to walk off the ship by himself.

"Then find another shop," Arnold said, "or buy one of these bad boys for 500,000 gold debloons."

"We'll take the ship over there, but we won't pay with debloons," Rick said pointing to the biggest ship of the bunch.

"No money. No ship." Arnold curtly replied.

"Oh no you misunderstand. I meant we won't pay you with gold but what about making you a part of our crew as payment? We need a new repairman since Cutlass fired ours." Rick realized he hit the jackpot when he saw Arnold's face light up.

"You got yourself a deal!" Arnold at once agreed. He hated paying Proper taxes, they were expensive and horrible. Plus, years of repairing pirate ships made him long for adventures on the high sea. The entire crew stared at Arnold's head-scratching deal with their mouths open.

"Well then, let's go," Rick said, feeling happy about the deal he made. This surely was a sign he was meant to be a captain someday. "The ship's gotta name?" He asked.

"Pintaloon's Revenge. And it's fully stocked with weapons, cannons, food and lots to drink." Arnold gleefully replied. Turns out Arnold had prepared the ship as tax payment to the Propers and he loaded it up with extra supplies, so they wouldn't bother him for another month.

"That's a fine name for such a sturdy looking ship. Hope it holds up better than the Plunderer." Rick said.

They unloaded their supplies from the Plunderer and tied the Grouper to the back of the Pintaloon's Revenge. Before anyone could celebrate, Brunt shouted from the dock, "Blackblade's minion ship that was following us since before King Crab Island has caught up with us."

"Let's get the Pintaloon's Revenge sailing and attack!" Cutlass commanded. He thought it unlikely Blackblade would be on a minion ship which meant they could easily get away.

Cutlass's crew successfully attacked the ship causing it to sink and within minutes they were safely continuing their course to find the next medallion.

High Seas

Amazing things began happening to Rick after boarding Pintaloon's Revenge. The crew started treating him with respect. Most just gave simple compliments like, "nice work out there junior" and "you really outdid yourself this time kid" but a few helped him swab the decks and taught him to catch sharks and cobblers (a type of massive fish). Rick was even allowed in the main cabin permanently.

The ultimate reward came four hours later when Cutlass walked towards Rick grabbed Tugger's hat and placed it on Rick. "Well done, first mate," Cutlass said. Rick had never been happier in his life. Things could not have been better.

Chapter 7:
Sky-High

The Race Begins

"Sir, we're approaching the Floating Islands," Brunt said.

"The what?" Rick said confused.

"The Floating Islands. They mysteriously float fifty meters above the Sea of Skull. No one knows why they float. The largest of the islands is believed to house a creature who guards one of the medallions. All we need to do is climb up fifty meters, grab the medallion and head to the next location. Easy peesy." Cutlass explained, making it all seem effortless.

"Don't forget we have to evade enemy fire too," Rick said, pointed to the Dark Serpent docked next to the center island.

To Cutlass's surprise, Blackblade had beat them to the Floating Island. *The battle with the minion ship was merely a distraction to slow us down! Wait! Could it be that Blackblade knows the Circle of Justice will lead him to the portal? That's it! He also wants the medallions, but it's not the treasure Blackblade is after, it's the mystic. He wants total power and if he gets a mystic he could use its magic to take over Reefia!*

The Pintaloon's Revenge sailed straight towards the middle Floating Island where the Dark Serpent docked. On the Dark Serpent was a long ladder, large enough to stow away in the ship's hull. The ladder was not tall enough to go all the way to the Floating Islands, but the crew had attached smaller ladders to make one extremely long ladder. Blackblade must have already gone up with some of his crew mates because there was no sign of him on the Dark Serpent. The rest of the crew appears to have stayed behind because there was a lot of laughter coming from the bottom decks of the ship. They seemed to be partying, leaving the deck clear of people.

"That makes things 45% easier for us," Rick said. "We can climb their ladder too."

"Make it 35% easier first mate," Mahanti cautioned. "We first have to board the Dark Serpent to get to the ladder."

Cutlass, Rick, Timmy, Brunt, Tugger and Mahanti, boarded the Dark Serpent without anyone seeing them. Rick noticed that Mahanti seemed happier on the Dark

Serpent then on the Pintaloon's Revenge, he also knew his way around better than the crew.

Up, Up, Up, and Away

This is what Rick said to himself as he climbed the endlessly long ladder. Around one hour later they had reached the top. The Floating Islands had beautiful waterfalls, springs, dense jungles and weird wildlife everywhere. Birds of all shapes and sizes were in nests and flying all about. Winged lizards where buzzing by. Rick soon realized most of the wildlife had wings and could fly. Even the fish in the springs could glide. The Floating Islands were magical wonderlands.

Find It, Find It

This is what Cutlass and his crew heard from Blackblade as they crouched behind a big green leafed bush.

"Ahhh you two morons. I said find the medallion not a metal. And he's the first mate with the badge. Ugh! I cannot believe I brought two morons with me instead of my second mate. C'mon hurry up. Cutlass is not far behind. His ship is coming this way. Hurry!" Blackblade at once ran out of the bush and into the jungle. The two morons ran behind him and the rest of the crew followed.

An Epic Sky-Fight

"Now's our chance," Rick said. "We simply follow them, and they'll lead us to the medallion. We get the medallion, fight the beast, and run back down the ladder to the Dark Serpent then back to our ship."

"Good plan," Cutlass whispered as he got up and followed Blackblade's men.

Around five minutes had passed when they heard one of the men who had climbed up a tree yell excitedly, "Look what I found in this giant eagle's nest." The nest was so large the man looked like a dwarf next to it. He held up the medallion then placed it back down as Blackblade and his crew quickly made their way up the tree towards the nest. To Blackblade's surprise, Cutlass and his crew emerged from the forest and were climbing trees nearby heading towards the nest all the while firing their pistols. Blackblade realized Cutlass might reach the medallion before him so he told his men to focus on fighting Cutlass's crew and told one of the morons to grab the medallion. Cutlass was at that moment saying the same thing to Rick.

Rick climbed up the sturdiest branch got inside the nest and ran towards the medallion which was on the other side of the nest. Inside the nest there was a strange pile of gold feathery plates. The moron was right behind. He pulled out his sword and ran towards Rick. The two were engaged in an intense battle when suddenly, they heard the shrill squawk of a bird so loud it could make glass shatter. Before either of them could react, the feathery gold plates beneath them moved up and up until there was a humongous golden eagle under their feet. The moron at once fainted beside Rick. The golden eagle started to attack, firing its plate-like feathers and killing several of Blackblade's men. Rick quickly ran towards the medallion but was stopped in his tracks by the sound of gunshot close to his head **"bam!"** It was Blackblade firing at him. Rick turned to see Blackblade running towards him, sword in the air. Rick continued running towards the medallion. Blackblade was so close he was in arm's reach. Just then the golden eagle turned its head, plucked Blackblade up and threw him out of the nest sending him flying into a palm tree. He was still alive and heading back to get the medallion.

Rick estimated he had a good five minutes until Blackblade got to him. He ran as fast as he could, grabbed the medallion and headed to the ladder, but before he could get out of the nest the golden eagle grabbed him by his shirt and flew away with him. The eagle flew to the most elevated part of the Floating Islands where it would be difficult for any pirates to reach them.

The golden eagle put Rick on the ground then asked, "Why did you steal the medallion?"

"It's a long story but the short answer is the medallion is necessary to find a bigger treasure." Rick replied puzzled by the question. "Why are you asking? Isn't your purpose to kill the enemy instantly?

"Fair point. The reason I ask is that you remind me of someone from the Avatorios family."

"Well I am. Does that mean you won't kill me?"

"Avatorios gave me a medallion and asked me to protect it so why would I kill his kind if he gave me this responsibility?"

"I'm really confused. Are you going to kill me or not?"

"Of course not! You are Avatorios's family, not some scallywag from the Western Pirate Clan, plus Avatorios himself told me that a boy from his bloodline would find all seven medallions."

"I'm that boy?" Rick said with disbelief.

"I imagine so---"

Before the golden eagle could say anything more, Rick was for a split second deafened by the biggest bang he had ever heard. The golden eagle fell dead. Behind the eagle were 80 men with muskets, pistols and even some cannons. It was Blackblade and his crew. Rick expected he was about to die. The men reloaded their guns and aimed at Rick, but before they could pull the trigger, Cutlass stormed in with his crew.

fighting in the Sky

Soon enough Rick could see Dunchest, Wheeler, Brunt, Tugger, Nettle, who surprisingly was very good at fighting, also Morano and his fishing crew, the new second mate Brakius (the ship's minotaur), Griger (the ship's lizard man), Fin, Mahanti and many others. Rick felt relieved to see them all. He drew his sword, the medallion safely in a pouch around his waist, and ran to join the fight. Something though was very strange. Blackblade's crew was a tough force, especially Blackblade who was full of energy unlike Cutlass and his crew. There was no winning this battle thought Rick. He needed a new plan, and quickly. They ran to the ladder but Blackblade's men were right behind them and others were coming up the ladder. There was only one solution: **JUMP**!

Cutlass, Rick and the rest of the crew jumped off the island into the water below. They all swam to the Pintaloon's Revenge, narrowly escaping death and sailing as fast as possible away from the Floating Islands.

Chapter 8:
Three Cheers for Rick

Chug Chug Chug Chug

Rick sat down at the big oval table below deck enjoying a delicious feast with the crew. Nettle and Chef Nico had made lots of dishes, like cobbler soup and chicken wings with Tunerberry sauce. The largest dish in the feast was roasted turkey with a side of mashed potatoes and tropical mangoes. Rick received many gifts for getting the medallion. Cutlass gave him a new sword just his size, Brakius gave him a musket, and Morano gave him new clothes that made him look as grand as a first mate. Tugger gave him a special lucky feather for his hat, Fin gave him a book on fighting, and Griger gave him a special lizard-styled knife. The only one who didn't give him a gift was Mahanti. He didn't even come to the feast.

Trial By Fire

When Rick realized Mahanti wasn't there, he snuck out of the party room to go look for him. He didn't want Cutlass to make a big commotion about Mahanti not being there. He checked the sleeping chambers, the shock locker (aka cannon ball storage) and the kitchen-- only Chef Nico was there making a cake for the feast. Rick loved Nico since he gave him food whenever he wanted. Rick then went to the sleep quarters, the stinky toilets, fuel storage room, and the weapons room where they stored cutlasses, swords, pistols and muskets stolen from the Propers. There were barrels and barrels of gunpowder and cannon balls too, but no Mahanti to be found. Then Rick went to the deck of the ship. There, he saw Mahanti at the bow side next to a mail pelican who delivers mail over the sea. Mahanti was holding a letter and intently reading it. Rick was puzzled. Barely anyone got letters, and who would contact Mahanti he wondered. Mahanti's entire family was killed by the Propertorian army during one of the many wars fought in the Crystal Sea. His home town was destroyed and he was the only survivor. Rick decided he would find out. He went over to Mahanti, tapped his shoulder, and asked what he was reading. Mahanti was startled and hid the letter under his shirt.

"Nothing, just... just... reading," Mahanti stammered with an odd look on his face.

"Nothing? There's a great party downstairs, you're absent and a mail pelican is sitting next to you," Rick said pointing out the obvious.

Right then Cutlass walked onto the deck. "Rick, there you are. What happened?"

"I was looking for Mahanti but he's acting suspicious," Rick said.

"Hahahahhah, good one Rick. Mahanti is the most trustworthy pirate ever, don't be silly."

"But then why is he secretly reading a letter and who is it from if his entire family is dead."

"You're right lad. Mahanti, what are ya hidin from me?"

Mahanti quickly jumped off the boat, grabbed a cannon sticking out of one of its slots and swung from cannon to cannon until he was at the far back of the ship, then jumped in the dinghy tied to the back of Pintaloon's Revenge. Cutlass ran after Mahanti, pulling him out of the dinghy by his shirt.

"I said what are ya hidin from me?" Cutlass said angrily.

"N n n nothing sir, nothing?" Mahanti replied, scared as ever.

"Ya right, ya never get mail, ya know what, let's do a trial right here right now."

Soon enough, the entire crew was on deck, torches where lit and the ship illuminated. Mahanti was tied to the main mast in the center of the ship. Fin and Griger both guarded Mahanti so that he could not escape. Brakius brought up a few torture devices in case they where needed to make Mahanti tell the truth. Everyone was chanting, "**trial by fire**!"

"We come here for the trial of Mahanti, for being oddly suspicious and trying to escape the ship. Our witness Rick will take it from here," Cutlass said.

"Well you see," Rick said, "Mahanti was reading mail secretly. First, he never gets mail and second who would send him mail."

"Okay boys, he's got a letter, search him for it." Cutlass ordered.

"Aha I found something," Griger said, holding a piece of paper in his hand.

On the Paper

Mahanti, it's Blackblade. We were defeated the other day by that doo-doo face Cutlass. I need you to steal the medallions, escape without being seen and bring them to me. Good luck my super sly spy.

Super Sly Spy

The entire crew was shocked.

"Is Blackblade on trial for using potty humor in his letter?" Nico asked.

"Noooooo!! You dim wit, Mahanti is a spy," Cutlass replied exasperated.

"Blackblade writes in potty humor. That's so un-pirate like, no?" Nico teased, as laughter erupted from the crew.

"Shut up, this is important," Cutlass said.

"Not as important as Blackblade writing in potty humor," Timmy said joining in.

"Hahahahaha!" Laughed the crew again.

"I can't believe my crew is made up of idiots!" Cutlass said frustrated. Soon the laughing was over. It was time for the torture to begin. Brakius untied Mahanti from the main sail and placed him on a device used for ripping people in half known as the **rack**. He tied ropes to Mahanti's feet and arms and started twisting the rack.

"Aaaahhhh the pain! I'll tell, I'll tell whatever you want, just stop."

"Spill it or we'll rip ya apart," Cutlass angrily shouted.

"Okay, okay. I think Blackblade is trying to find a mystic. They have magical powers and under his rule they could help him dominate Reefia in no time."

"I already figured that out fish lips. Brakius, keep going." Cutlass said.

"Right o, boss," Brakius said as he kept turning the crank until Mahanti was about to rip apart. Just then Brakius stopped.

"Um boss. Am I allowed to use more torture devices than just the rack?"

"Go ahead, he's an evil spy!" Cutlass replied as he went to the main cabin leaving Brakius to continue his torturing.

A short while later Cutlass returned to the deck but there was no sign of Mahanti.

"Where are his remains?" Cutlass asked puzzled.

"Don't know, don't care. My job here is done." Brakius answered, as he put away the torture devices. "He disappeared before he was about to have a deadly ice bath, but he did go into the incinerating cage so I am guessing he's dead." Brakius sounded very confident, but Cutlass wasn't so sure.

Chapter 9:
A Pesky Brat

Where's My Pay?

"Well," said Mahanti, "aren't you going to pay me?"

"Ye got the medallions, right?" Blackblade eagerly asked.

"Ummm, not quiet. I kinda spilled the beans after Cutlass tortured me."

"Then of course there is no payment!" Blackblade shouted. "You spilled the beans so you don't get paid. The beans are spilled! Do you not understand me? You double crossing---! Even though I would like to throw you off my ship, it occurs to me you can still be useful for something."

"Like what?" Mahanti asked relieved to know he would be alive a bit longer.

"What do you know about crystal balls? We are going to have a little chat with the Propers." Blackblade said.

Bait, Bait, Bait, Bait, Bait, Bait, Bait

"Captain, there are no fish in this area," Morano said.

"That's a good sign. It means we're getting close to the Volcanic Archipelago Islands," Cutlass said with glee.

"Capitano, you may want to see this," Timmy said. "The Propers are blockading the islands."

"But why?" Rick asked. "They only want to rule Reefia and eliminate all pirates. The Volcanic Archipelago is no use to them."

"It's because of me," Cutlass responded. "The Propers have been trying to eliminate the Southern Pirate captain for years."

"For some reason I doubt that," said Alec, the ship's know-it-all. Alec was a smarty pants at everything besides fighting so he was barley in on all the action. "The Propers like surrounding their enemies, not blocking them from their goals."

"Right ye are," suddenly came a voice from Mahanti's crystal ball which was in a heap of junk on the floor of the deck. It was Blackblade's voice. "I hired the Propers to surround the island, promising them gold and you in return, if you survive. Ha Ha Ha!"

"But how?" Rick asked, astonished to hear Blackblade's voice coming from the crystal ball.

"I used Mahanti to send a message. I know they've been trying to capture Cutlass for years. Now's their chance. Fire at will general." Blackblade commanded.

At that moment, several loud bangs could be heard from the Proper ships. A third of the Pintaloon's Revenge's deck was splintered to bits.

"Awwwww come on. This is a new ship. Arnold, I thought you said this ship couldn't be destroyed?" Cutlass said disappointedly.

"Captain, we can't beat an entire Proper fleet!" Arnold replied.

"That's the least of our worries. We're about to be bait for sharks! Load the cannons!" Tugger yelled.

Soon enough Pintaloon's Revenge was blasting the enemy. **1, 2, 3** went the ships, each going down after the other, sinking to their doom. Then came a bigger, tougher ship with around 80 cannons. Pintaloon's Revenge didn't stand a chance. Before long, the Propertorian sailors boarded Pintaloon's Revenge shooting and slashing everyone in sight. Alec was injured in the leg. Falling to the ground he cried out, "Someone save me!"

Captainsparkles, the crew's aged parrot was the only one to come.

"Captainsparkles, give me the gunpowder so I can shoot the enemy," Alec gasped.

"Squawk, squawk. Abandon ship, squawk, abandon ship, squawk!" Captainsparkles said as he flew away.

"Noooooooooooo!" Alec screamed as a Propertorian soldier killed him.

Only a third of Pintaloon's Revenge's crew got away: Cutlass, Rick, Fin, Brakius, Griger, Nettle, Morano, Nico, Mig, Brunt, Timmy, Arnold, Dunchest, Wheeler and Captainsparkles. Rick grabbed the three medallions on their way out. They abandoned Pintaloon's Revenge and sailed away on the Grouper to the nearest Southern Pirate Clan island where they stayed for a day until finally deciding to steal a big schooner. It was blue and at least thirty feet long with a steering wheel instead of a tiller. They called it the Slick Devil. It was so fast when they stole it the owner couldn't even catch up using his neighbor's boat.

The other good thing was the Slick Devil could house a crew and not a tiny family like the Grouper. The ship was also well armed and had more powerful cannons. It had ten muskets and twenty pistols all in racks in the storage room. There was even a sharpener for swords and cutlasses. The crew thought that the ship was a tad bit better than Pintaloon's Revenge. Best of all, they had a new ship, so the Propertorians wouldn't recognize them, plus everyone thought they were dead anyway.

Back on Track

The crew was back on course toward the Volcanic Archipelago Islands to get the next medallion when they saw the Dark Serpent docked on one of the islands. Through the spyglass they could see Blackblade, his crew and the traitor Mahanti clambering up rocky volcanoes to the biggest volcano of them all.

"We gotta get there before them, otherwise they'll kill us. Remember we don't have a full crew," Rick said.

"Ya scallywags," Cutlass yelled at the crew. "Ya heard Rick, now dock on the other side of the island so they don't see us."

"Err Captain, Blackblade is headin up the big volcano just as we speak," Fin said, looking through the spyglass.

"Well then get the buckets, come on, hurry up ya scallywags," Cutlass said, jumping off the boat with the crew following behind. They climbed up the other side of the volcano. At the top of the volcano there was a hole overflowing with burning lava that extended all the way down to the center of the earth, or so they thought. Blackblade wasn't there and neither was his crew. It appeared Blackblade mistakenly took the long route.

"Hmmm, that's strange," Cutlass said in a suspicious tone.

"Where's the dragon? Shouldn't it be here?" Brakius said.

"It's a Lava Dragon which means it's swimming in the lava," Nico said.

"Shut up, I'm trying to think," Cutlass blurted out.

"Wait, I've got it," Griger shouted excitedly. He took a pail of water then poured it into the lava but to everyone's surprise, the water went right through the lava and down the hole. The lava didn't sizzle, nor did it turn to rock.

"What just happened?" Nettle said looking quite puzzled.

"It's an illusion," Griger said. The volcano is made to look like lava is flowing from it but there's nothing there."

Everyone jumped in the hole and landed with a **thump**.

Chapter 10:
Den of the Lava Dragon

Death, Fire and Lava

The Lava Dragon was asleep deep in the volcano, snorting and snoring so hard it sounded like loud growls. Just then Cutlass's crew heard mumbles of a captain yelling at his crew from the top of the volcano. He said, "C'mon scallywags, especially ye lassies."

Timmy accidently stepped on the Lava Dragon's tail. The dragon roared loudly and grabbed Nico and Timmy with its claws, but then it took one look at Rick and started to purr (if a soft growl could be considered a purr). Suddenly, they heard the voice of Mahanti saying to Blackblade's crew, "Hey guys the volcano is an illusion." Soon enough Blackblade's crew came tumbling in, landing in a big heap.

"What? Cutlass? I thought ye where dead. Well who cares you're good as dead now!" Blackblade fired his pistol at Cutlass who quickly dodged the bullet, which instead hit the dragon. The Lava Dragon stood up growling and blew a plume of fire at Blackblade. Then the Lava Dragon made a huge jump and tried to pounce (just imagine a cat and you're a mouse and this cat breathes fire and lives in a volcano, well this is what they are experiencing). The volcano started to shake.

"Captain, the volcano is about to erupt. **RUN!**" Griger said.

"But didn't Mahanti say this was an illusion of a volcano," Cutlass said unsure of what was going on.

"Well, there still could be lava under us even if there is no lava in the volcanic hole," Griger said.

Rick noticed the dragon seemed to be using its talons to point at its back. "I think the dragon is telling us to hitch a ride on its back out of here," Rick said. The crew jumped on the dragon's back. It flew **up, up, up** and out of the volcano just as it erupted. The dragon then held out its talon. On it was the reason Cutlass's crew came here in the first place: another medallion! Rick was amazed that one of the creatures guarding a medallion was now helping him. He decided to name the dragon Heatbreath.

"Squawk squawk, abandon dragon, abandon dragon!" Captainsparkles protested. He was afraid of dragons, believing they were predators.

"Oh no ye don't," Cutlass said, grabbing the parrot's tail.

"Squawk squawk, killer killer, squawk," Captainsparkles repeated as Cutlass quickly covered the parrot's beak. Heatbreath landed on the Slick Devil and everyone jumped off his back and headed to their posts.

"Now where to?" Wheeler asked excitedly awaiting their next adventure.

"To the Whirlpool of Ultimate Doom," Cutlass answered.

"What is that and where is it?" Wheeler said confused.

"I don't know," Cutlass said with a shrug, "but I've heard from the tales of pirates that another medallion is to be found there."

Heatbreath pointed one of his talons North. "I think he's pointing to Savage Penguin Island. Wait, nope, somewhere else?" Wheeler asked trying to guess what Heatbreath meant.

"A long time ago, before Blackblade was captain, Propers sailed near the Western Pirate Clan and guess what happened?" Cutlass said in suspense.

"They came back with lots of gold because the prior captain was extremely generous?" Wheeler asked.

"No, they never came back. Most pirates believe they were eaten by the Kraken who lives in the middle of the Whirlpool of Ultimate Doom. The whirlpool is 150 yards wide. Not a soul survives the Kraken. It loves humans.

The Kraken is not like the golden eagle or Heatbreath. It doesn't care whether you're related to Avatorios. All it wants to do is eat ye. It took two weeks for our ancestor to put the medallion on one of its tentacles. Avatorios lost his leg, hand and one eye in the process. We may not survive the trip to the Whirlpool of Ultimate Doom, but we must try." Cutlass said.

The Mahanti Machine

"Su nu wut cup tun," said one of the two morons in Blackblade's crew.

"We find out where Cutlass and his crew went," Blackblade replied, impatient to get going.

"But they died, no?"

"You moron! They were just here flying on a dragon's back when we were about to be toast until Mahanti used his magic to save us. Now we'll use Mahanti's magic to find them," Blackblade replied excitedly.

"How?" Asked the other moron.

"Like this, hit it Bruty." Blackblade replied.

Bruty pulled a lever near the mast and in came Mahanti tied up in ropes (*You're likely wondering why is he tied up, isn't he useful to Blackblade? Well, Blackblade knows he's useful but is punishing Mahanti because he can't do his job correctly*). Blackblade commanded Mahanti to cast a spell that would allow Blackblade to see and hear Cutlass's conversation with Wheeler.

"They are headin' to the Kraken," Blackblade gathered from listening to the conversation. "Jackpot! They are also in the Crystal Sea, not far from us. Let's get 'em, hurry!"

Peace on the High Seas

"Can you believe it," Rick said with delight, "we've got four medallions and a new dragon friend. Plus, the sea is so calm Wheeler doesn't have to steer Slick Devil. He can relax with us. How about some dinner Great Uncle? Wheeler, tell everyone to meet on deck for a banquet."

Wheeler ran to get the rest of the crew. The Southern Pirate Clan rarely had banquets until they began finding medallions. This time around, Nico and Nettle prepared a surprisingly large amount of food. There was even a pile of dead cows and chickens for Heatbreath to gnaw on. Dessert though was the best. Chocolate fish ice cream and strawberry filled pie with Chichiberries (sweet tropical berries from Coconut Island). The pie was so humongous even Heatbreath would take a long time to eat it all. The crew feasted for two weeks, eating 28 desserts, until they had mega belly aches! Rick had never been so happy.

Chapter 11:
𝕸𝖍𝖎𝖗𝖑𝖕𝖔𝖔𝖑 𝖔𝖋 𝖀𝖑𝖙𝖎𝖒𝖆𝖙𝖊 𝕯𝖔𝖔𝖒

Doom, Doom, Doom...

An awkward silence filled the air as the crew looked suspiciously at the Whirlpool of Ultimate Doom. They were wondering why there was no Kraken in it when suddenly, a gigantic purple octopus-like creature, with a pink underside popped out of nowhere. It was floating upside down for ease of grabbing and eating prey. Its tentacles looked like it could reach past the edge of the Whirlpool and still reach a ship 300 yards away. **The Kraken**!

"Ready the sails men. Load the cannons. We're about to get a beating by the Kraken. Wheeler, try to circle around the Whirlpool," Cutlass shouted.

Just then, a large tentacle arose from the water grabbing the Slick Devil's mast. Cutlass fired his pistol but the Kraken didn't even react. The Kraken threw the Slick

Devil into the air as the crew fired all their weapons. The Kraken was still unhurt. Suddenly, they heard shouts of, "**fire, fire**" coming from the western side of the ship. It was the Dark Serpent! The crew had run out of ammunition and were sitting ducks out there. There was no way to escape. They were all dooooooooooomed!

Idea of a Century

Just then Rick had an idea. He ran to Cutlass and grabbed a book of folk tales from his pocket. He zipped through the pages until he came to a section about Krakens. It said Krakens are thought to be vulnerable to heat, but this seemed doubtful to him since Krakens lived in water. But it was worth a try, he thought. He asked Cutlass if they had any whale oil.

"Aye, that we do," Cutlass said.

Rick poured whale oil into a small dinghy attached to the back of the ship and with Heatbreath's help, flew with the dinghy and dropped it onto the Kraken while firing a jet of flames at the dinghy. The dinghy hit the Kraken where it was most vulnerable: its mouth. The Kraken thought he was eating a ship and greedily devoured it. There was a loud shriek and then a burst of fire shot out of his mouth, followed by a plume of smoke. The crew couldn't believe it, the Kraken had swallowed the burning dinghy.

KABOOM! The dinghy exploded inside the Kraken. He sank to the bottom of the Crystal Sea and the Whirlpool of Ultimate Doom faded away. As the Kraken died, one of its tentacles flung something at a nearby island. It was the medallion they came for. Cutlass's crew heard Blackblade on the Dark Serpent yelling, "go, go, go, get that medallion."

Rick told Heatbreath to fire into the water close to the back of the Slick Devil to create a large wave that would push the ship to the island faster. They were only meters away from next medallion. Unfortunately, so was Blackblade. The two crews ran towards the medallion, but Rick got there first, thanks to a ride on Heatbreath's back. He took the medallion, held it up in the light and told his crew to get on the dragon. Right then Timmy saw a large ship. It was one of the backup crews from the Southern Pirate Clan.

"I knew the backup crew would reach us!" Cutlass said, happy to get some help and a new ship. They abandoned the Slick Devil and boarded the larger ship called Plunderer's Revenge. The ship was medium size, had at least 25 cannons and a big mast with a huge sail. The ship had a new crew, plus to Cutlass's surprise, two of his friends, Mort the Mute and Crine the Cute. Cutlass and Rick took control of the ship. Dunchest and Heatbreath pointed to the next target and they set sail North.

In the distance, they could hear Blackblade scream-ing at his crew. "You idiots, we lost a medallion again!"

Mad, Mad, Mad, Mad

"I hate all of you, "Blackblade shouted. "I should've killed all of you. So, I will."

"But ye can't," said a crewmate, "the curse made us hard to kill."

"Not if I stab ye to death with the Ebony Blade. **Run!**"

The crew tried to run for their lives but Blackblade killed all of them except for a few he liked or those that hid from the Ebony Blade. The two morons sadly were not part of the crew who died. Blackblade did not fol-low Cutlass's new ship, the Plunderer's Revenge. Instead, he headed to Dark Wood, a Western Pirate town, to get the Elite Dark Men, Blackblade's main and best army of pirates. These men were trained to kill even the most for-midable foe. Blackblade was going to use them to finally defeat Cutlass.

Chapter 12:
Welcome to Savage Penguin Land

Savage Penguins

Cutlass's crew set sail for Savage Penguin Land where the next medallion awaited them. They passed through the Strait of Craziness arriving at the island.

"Gentlemen," Cutlass said, "welcome to Savage Penguin Island, where cute penguins are savage, talk like babies, and Wallrusters rule."

Wallrusters are walruses with tusks forged from scrap metal. These tusks are extremely hard, sharp and junky looking.

The crew stared at the penguins. They had tiny pick-axes but still looked cute.

"They don't look so savage," said Domenden the crew's scaredy-cat. "They look quite cu--- aahh get 'em off me! Get 'em off me!" A Savage Penguin had jumped on Domenden, hitting him with its pickaxe. Then another penguin appeared at the wheel of the ship. Soon, hundreds of savage penguins took control of Plunderer's Revenge.

"Off we go to King Fatdipper. He'll settle this," said the Savage Penguin at the wheel in an adorable yet frightening voice.

King of the Savage Penguins

The penguins docked at Panic Bay and waddled over to a camp with many more cute but Savage Penguins. In the center of the camp there was a large ditch with huge piles of treasure. Rick wanted to kill the king and steal all the treasure for himself. But that was not his mission. In the center of the ditch there was an ice throne surrounded by treasure. On it sat a giant, fat penguin as big as Rick.

"Me nem is King Fat-dip-paw," said King Fatdipper in his most gangster voice. "Ja rule here."

"Ye don't happen to know about the medallions that open the Circle of Justice?"

"Ja man, me know everything," King Fatdipper replied.

"You seem depressed," Rick said.

"I am," said King Fatdipper. "There's a creature on the coast eatin' all me Savage Penguin sons."

"Sons?" Rick said astonished.

"Of course! Everyone here part of me family. The wife, she lay 25,000 eggs every year until she die in child birth not too long ago."

"Sad," Cutlass said.

"Tell ya what," Fatdipper said, "I'll make ya a deal."

Savage Penguins Make a Deal

"If you defeat the Wallruster, I'll give you this!" Fatdipper said, pulling out a shiny medallion from his treasure pile.

"Where'd ye get that?" Cutlass said trying not to seem too excited.

"'Bout four moons ago, some of me sons survived one Wallruster attack and bring me back dis here medallion."

"What an odd twist of events. We came here expecting to kill the beast and get the medallion, not kill the beast for someone else who might not even give us the medallion," Cutlass lamented.

"It's the same thing," Rick said. "We still have to fight the Wallruster to get the medallion. Besides, we're pirates, so what does it matter who we fight so long as King Fatdipper keeps his word."

"Alright fine. King Fatdipper, you've got yourself a deal. You better not go back on your word or we'll be fighting you too." Cutlass said.

Chapter 13:
The Wallrusters

How Hard Can This Be?

"How hard can this be?" Rick said. "All we have to do is kill the Wallruster, grab the medallion, then be home in time for lunch, right?"

"Ye haven't heard the legends have ye," said the new pirate swabbing the deck. The crew called him Swabber.

Mort the Mute nodded in agreement. He made a sign that only a few members of the crew could understand. "About 76 years ago," he signed, "a huge walrus with metal tusks ate Captain Peg, the leader of the Eastern Pirate Clan. Peg's death caused great distress among his clan and made it easy for the rising Proper Empire to defeat them. If not for the Wallrusters, the Eastern Pirate Clan would still have control of the entire bottom half of the Propertorian Empire."

"In that case, Rick, why don't you lead the battle against the Wallrusters," Cutlass quickly responded, concerned he might have the same fate as Captain Peg.

"Uh, sure, if you say so," Rick said hesitantly. Just then, **ding**, he had an idea!

Another Great Idea

"What's the plan for defeating the Wallrusters?" Captain Cutlass asked impatient to get going.

Before Rick could answer, Crine the Cute chimed in. "Daddy look, a baby elephant seal." Crine said, referring to Rick who tended to him more than anyone else on the ship. "Can I keep him?" Just then, a giant Wallruster snuck up behind the seal eating it. "**Waaaaaahhhhh!** Daddy, stomp that Wallruster." Crine cried out.

Rick's grand idea was to strap a cannon on Heatbreath, fly to the Wallruster, fire up the cannon and shoot cannon balls at the Wallruster.

"Alright, let's do this," Rick said, climbing on top of Heatbreath to begin securing a cannon.

"Um Rick, you may want to see this," Cutlass signaled.

"See wha...wow?" Rick gasped in shock looking at the coast. There were a dozen Wallrusters awaiting them.

"Uh-Oh this is bad," Rick whispered to himself. "Plan B, to the ship!" Rick ran to the ship with the crew following behind. Everyone boarded the ship as quickly as possible.

"And what now?" Cutlass asked.

"We shoot cannons at them," Timmy suggested.

"Good plan," Rick said in agreement. Soon enough he readied Plunderer's Revenge to fire.

"Ready, set, fire," Cutlass commanded. Plunderer's Revenge fired cannon balls in all directions, but they hit nothing. Wallrusters in the meantime swam from the coast to the ship and were using their tusks to poke holes in it.

"Make for the sails, we must head for a safer place!" Cutlass directed the crew.

"Hey, I have another idea. Let's head for the junky island over there covered with scrap metal," Rick said.

While Plunderer's Revenge was sailed towards the island, Mort the Mute was signing desperately without luck to get Cutlass's attention.

Scrap Metal Island

"Ah, safe at last," Cutlass said, as Plunderer's Revenge docked at the island of junk, also known by pirates as Scrap Metal Island.

"Great Uncle, uh, you might want to look at what's waiting for us." Rick said, pointing to 100 juvenile Wallrusters, plus the king and queen Wallrusters emerging from a heap of scrap metal growling at the Plunderer. Some of the juveniles already began chomping holes in the ship's side. Meanwhile, Mort the Mute continued making lots of disturbing and confusing hand signals when finally, Cutlass took notice asking the Translator to translate what Mute was saying.

The Translator took a deep breath and conveyed Mute's words in a loud voice to match Mute's rapid hand signals. "I HAVE BEEN TELLING YOU OVER AND OVER, THIS IS SCRAP METAL ISLAND. WHY ARE WE AT AN ISLAND WHERE WALLRUSTERS GO TO BUILD THEIR TUSKS?!"

"Ooohhh, that's what you were saying!" The entire crew said in unison.

"Now what do we do?" Griger asked. "How are we going to defeat a whole bunch of Wallrusters?"

"Easy, Heatbreath is our secret weapon," Rick said confidently, as he mounted the dragon and headed towards the island.

An Epic Success

Heatbreath fired a large blast of flames engulfing parts of Scrap Metal Island and killing a bunch of Wallrusters in the process. **Shoom**, **Shoom**, **Shoom**. Heatbreath fired several more blasts at the king and queen but other Wallrusters protected them by jumping in the way.

"Fire! Ye swashbucklin' excuse for a crew!" Cutlass yelled. With no backup and the constant threat of cannonballs and dragon fire, the king and queen jumped in the water and headed straight for the Unknown Regions just before Heatbreath blew up Scrap Metal Island with his biggest, strongest blast of fire yet.

"Yay," Rick shouted gleefully. "Now we claim our next medallion from Fatdipper."

The Savage Penguins Say Goodbye

"Here you go, ye've earned it," Fatdipper said, handing the medallion to Rick.

The Savage Penguins in unison waved goodbye as the Plunderer's Revenge got ready to sail off. On board the ship, Crine the Cute really wanted to keep a penguin.

"Please let me keep a Savage Penguin, they're so cute," Crine pleaded as he picked up a penguin and hugged it. He hugged the penguin so hard all its stored weapons went flying into the air, some landing on Domenden.

"Aaahhh they're still savage, they're still savage!" Domenden cried out, after being hit another time by a pickaxe. Rick and Cutlass had a good laugh while setting sail to their next destination, Hydra Rock.

Short Break: Interview

Now I, Gromund, will do an interview with the Southern Pirate Clan's new ally, the Northern Pirates. If you haven't heard of these guys, they are like Vikings with old-fashioned bows and arrows and simple ships without cannons.

Gromund: How do you feel about your new ally, the Southern Pirates?

Northern Pirate: Those guys are really amazing.

Gromund: Why are they amazing?

Northern Pirate: They beat the impossible to defeat Wallruster. Now we own all the scrap metal on Scrap Metal Island!

Gromund: How do you feel about the Southern Pirate Clan using a fire dragon to kill the Wallrusters by blowing up Scrap Metal Island?

Awkward silence.

Northern Pirate: What's a fire dragon?

Gromund: Um, they're red giant flying reptiles that live inside volcanoes and breathe fire.

Northern Pirate: You mean like an ice dragon?

Gromund: No, I mean a dragon breathing fire, not ice.

Northern pirate: So, you mean like a lizard torch?

Gromund: Note to self, next time interview someone with a brain. Back to my story.

End of interview

Chapter 14:
Hydra Rock

The Rip Current

The Hydra Sea thrashed the Plunderer's Revenge everywhere. **Wooooosh** went the waves splashing the ship. There wasn't even a storm, just some drizzle, but large waves were coming at them from nowhere. The sea seemed to hate them.

"Arararar, aroooo," Dunchest howled. He hated the thrashing of the boat as did Captainsparkles.

"Squawk, we're gonna sink. Squawk, we're tipping. Squawk." Captainsparkles was so annoying, Wheeler fired a bullet into the air so he would shut up.

Suddenly, Wheeler noticed instead of going North they were going South. "Um Captain, we seem to be driftin' off course." Wheeler said, sounding stressed. The waves and winds are blowing us in the wrong direction."

"Well, I'm not the steering man, now am I?" Cutlass responded sarcastically.

"You're the Captain, you choose where we go, and right now we're going South." Wheeler snapped back defensively.

"I see where we are: The **Rip Currents**! We're drifting to where the Whirlpool of Ultimate Doom previously existed." Cutlass told his crew to change the sails in an unusual way so they caught more wind. He also made Heatbreath blow up barrels of gunpowder close to the ship thrusting it forward. It took hours of work, but they turned Northeast and went out of the Rip Current into a calmer but more mysterious part of the sea. The crew felt uneasy, they felt someone was watching from above, but it turns out they were being watched from deep below by millions of Sea Banshees. These were hideous gray hags with tattered tails who lured pirates to their death by mesmerizing them with shiny spheres of pearls which they placed on the water's surface. When the pirates reached for the pearls, the Sea Banshees would paralyze them with an awful shrieking scream then attack and eat them.

The Sea Banshees

Suddenly, there was a shimmer of light. "Look, beautiful floating pearls!" Brunt said excitedly.

"Don't be silly," Cutlass said. "There is no such thing as pearls floating in the sea." Before he could say anything else, some of the crew members hopped into a dinghy and went to collect the floating pearls. One crew member grabbed a pearl within arms' reach, but before he could bring his hand up, something grabbed him from below pulling him into the sea. The hideous creature screamed so loud the windows on the lower decks shattered, some of the men on the ship were paralyzed and more hideous creatures appeared grabbing all the men on the dinghy and pulled them under water. Soon, the water around the floating pearls was red with blood.

"What are these creatures?" Rick asked.

"Sea Banshees," Cutlass replied. "Summoned by the Thunder Hydra to keep trespassers away. They scream at ye, then eat ye when yer knocked out."

"How many are there?" Rick asked.

"According to legends, millions." Cutlass replied.

"How do we defeat them?" Rick asked.

"We please them with something that screams as loud as they do."

At that moment, the entire crew looked at the only baby on the ship: Crine the Cute. The crew began shouting, **"Sacrifice! Sacrifice! Sacrifice! Sacrifice! Sacrifice!"**

Before Rick could stop them, the crew threw Crine off the ship towards the Banshees. He landed on a nearby rock and began shrieking loudly.

The leader of the Sea Banshees, the largest one said, "One of ours is aboard that ship! Let them pass!"

The Sea Banshees moved aside for the Plunderer's Revenge to pass. Without anyone noticing and with Rick's help, Nico lowered a rope to the rock, climbed down and rescued Crine who was happy to be back on the ship.

The Largest Storm

Things seemed to get better for the crew. But then they heard a howling.

"More Sea Banshees?" Rick asked.

"No, much worse. Hurry below deck, we're in quite a storm." Cutlass replied. "Wheeler make sure the sails are flying with the wind. Not against it."

"Why would we want to go with the wind?" Rick asked, "Won't that just blow us off course?"

"Maybe, but I'm thinking the sails will pull us in the right direction if we let them." Cutlass replied. His theory was right. The ship sailed in circles for two minutes then went zigzaggedly on course. However, it was now raining hard. Water leaked through the wood and the wind create mini tsunamis on the deck. The crew was below deck afraid, watching, waiting, and listening for Wheeler's call.

After a while, Wheeler said, "All right ye can come out now. It's still stormy but nothing you guys can't handle." The sky was still full of gray clouds, it was raining, and there were some large waves, but not as bad as what they had just been through.

"There it is, Hydra Rock!" Rick exclaimed. The jagged rock, which was bigger than they had expected, had been hit by lightning many times. There was no vegetation on the island just charred black rock and a den visible to the crew upon docking the ship. They entered the den surprised to find it was full of treasure, but no sign of the Thunder Hydra. Gold, diamonds and amethyst were everywhere. The crew began stuffing their pockets, boots and shirts with treasure when Griger noticed a giant violet egg as tall as him. He wondered how big the Thunder Hydra was if the egg was this big. It meant the adult had to be huge! Just then they heard a roar.

Thunder Hydra

An unimaginably large head poked through a hole in the den's ceiling. It was bigger than Heatbreath, roaring with the force of a thousand earthquakes and shooting a bolt of purple-blue lightning at them in defense of its egg.

"Make for the ship!" Cutlass yelled. Rick thought he heard a hissing voice speaking into the den as he left. But that was impossible, he thought. Monsters can't speak.

The crew boarded the Plunderer's Revenge as fast as they could and sailed away from the den. Thunder Hydra finally showed itself. A huge body, shiny blue and purple, with a white underside, expansive wings and three giant heads attached to extremely long necks. It seemed to glow in the storm.

"Great Uncle, why are we turning away from Hydra Rock?" Rick asked confused.

"Oh, we're not going away from the beast. Turn the ship around Wheeler!"

Wheeler made a sharp turn and the Plunderer's Revenge sailed at top speed towards Thunder Hydra. "Yo, ho, ho!" Cutlass shouted with delight.

Thunder Hydra's heads roared and shot three bursts of lightning at the crew. The Plunderer's Revenge was badly damaged but still bolting towards the monster. Rick thought he heard the hissing voice again but this time from a farther distance.

Thunder Hydra jumped off Hydra Rock into the ocean creating a huge tidal wave then crawled back onshore to watch. The tidal wave almost knocked over the Plunderer's Revenge, but it quickly resettled. The entire crew was soaked.

"Keep goin' ye scrubby lot!" Cutlass yelled. "Show those heads what we're made of! Yo ho ho!"

Thunder Hydra created more waves, but the Plunderer's Revenge was still going until it was right in front of Hydra Rock. The middle head of Thunder Hydra zapped the entire crew knocking them all out, except Rick (and Heatbreath, but he wasn't on the ship at the time, so he didn't count). The middle head looked at Rick, opened its enormous jaws and swallowed him.

Belly of the Beast

Rick was in Thunder Hydra's stomach. After realizing its heart was at the base of the middle neck he came up with a plan. He drew his cutlass and walked up the slimy body of the beast.

It took him five minutes to reach the heart. He prepared for a jolt of energy and then swung his cutlass at the heart. There was a hard jerk, but the heart stayed untouched. Rick looked closer. There was an electrical field around the heart. Looks like Heatbreath is the only one who can save me now, he thought.

The Deal

Little did Rick know that Dracos, the family which dragons and hydras belong to, have a language called Draconis. Heatbreath had a plan. He was going to use Draconis to execute it.

"I'll make you a deal," Heatbreath said in Draconis. "If you give me Rick and the medallion, I'll--"

"Exactly what can you do to help us?" The middle head said suspiciously.

"You know Hydra eggs can only hatch under Dragon fire, right. If you give me what I asked for, I will hatch your egg."

"Deal!" Thunder Hydra replied happily.

Heatbreath dove into the den, lit up the egg, watched it crack, then zipped back up to Thunder Hydra. Out of the cracked egg crawled a one-headed miniature Hydra with lightening spikes.

"How about we name him Bolt?" Heatbreath suggested.

"Good choice," Thunder Hydra said nodding in agreement.

The middle head thanked Heatbreath, vomited Rick then used its talon to pluck a tooth from its jaw. On the tooth was another medallion. Now Rick had all seven medallions!

Success

The crew was just waking up when Rick arrived on top of Heatbreath.

"What in the name of Seven Seas just happened?" Cutlass asked.

"Heatbreath got the last medallion!" Rick said with delight.

The entire crew went up in cheers and Heatbreath and Thunder Hydra fired bolts of lightning and fire into the air. Everything was perfect now.

Chapter 15:

The Battle of Al-Cama

Two Messages

The Dark Serpent docked in the town of Dark Wood, in the land of the Western Pirate Clan. Blackblade came off the ship with some of his crew and walked into town. Drunk pirates were everywhere, shooting at walls and barrels of water. Some were setting houses on fire and laughing about it. Two stupid pirates where hitting each other with clubs and becoming stupider by the minute. Others were being shot out of cannons. Blackblade frolicked to the biggest place in the town of Dark Wood: **Elite Dark Men Manor**. To him, this was home. To Cutlass, this was a crazy place. To the King of the Propers, this was hell.

"DARK MEN ASSEMBLE," Blackblade commanded. At once, 1000 men came through the doors, down the stairs of the Manor and into the entrance where Blackblade was waiting. Dark Manor was so big the entire crew fit inside the front entrance.

"Who wants to kill Cutlass?" Blackblade shouted.

"We do," the Elite Dark Men responded in unison.

"Who wants to sink Cutlass's ship?"

"We do?" They again responded in unison.

"Who wants seven medallions?"

"Aaaaaaaaaaaaarrrrrrrrrrr we do?" They shouted for the 3rd time in unison.

"WHO WANTS TA KILL AN OLD ENEMY?" Blackblade said loudly.

"WE DO!" They again answered in unison.

"Well then come with me. Also, please stop saying everything in unison."

"Sorry." They again said in unison as Blackblade gave them a mean look.

Blackblade boarded the Elite Dark Men's ship known as the Elite Dark Serpent. He enlisted other ships to come until there where ten fully armed ships full of Western Pirates ready to fight. They all sailed off to meet the enemy.

Blackblade also got Mahanti to send a message to a Propertorian general asking if he could send troops to kill Cutlass since their last attempt at the volcanoes failed. The Propertorian general was mad about his failure to assassinate Cutlass at the volcanos, so he sent double the troops.

The Confrontation

The Plunderer's Revenge sailed out of the Hydra Sea. The crew waved goodbye to their new friends Thunder Hydra and its cute baby Bolt.

"Captain," Arnold yelled, "we seem to be headin' away from the Circle of Justice."

"We're out of supplies so we're going to Al-Cama, ye know the trading outpost. We can restock there." Cutlass replied.

Upon arriving at Al-Cama, the crew quickly walked across the dock to the shores. They were about to go onto the main path when all of a sudden, they heard: ***Click***. Four shotgun barrels were aimed at Cutlass.

"Ahoy travelers!" The person holding the gun said. He had a long black beard, was very muscular, and had a tattoo of a hydra eating a Wallruster, eating a Kraken, eating a Lava Dragon, eating a golden eagle, eating a Quetzal, eating a giant lobster.

"We faced all those peeps, except the Quetzal," Rick pointed out.

"I know, and do you know how I know? It's because I was there."

"Blackblade, it's you!" Cutlass gasped.

"Hi brother." Blackblade said with a grin.

Click *Click*. That was the sound of 10,000 Proper men aiming their pistols at Cutlass and his crew.

"Fire at will general." Blackblade shouted.

"**FIRE!**" Yelled a voice that sounded strangely familiar to Rick.

All the Propers and Elite Dark Men fired their guns killing 30 of Cutlass's men.

"Tell the men to load the cannons, sling yer guns and draw yer swords! We have a big battle ahead of us," Cutlass said to his men.

Fight to the Death

One of the Western Pirates lunged at Rick. Rick parried the lunge and returned the favor with a slash across the heart. The man died. Or at least Rick thought he died. He couldn't tell. From what he heard during his time at Antony Outpost, there was no way to know.

"All men to the ship! We are losing! We will have the upper hand with the cannons."

"Great Uncle, look!" Rick shouted.

Ten Viking-like ships sailed into the bay and started firing arrows. They didn't have the same technologies as the other pirate clans, but they were better fighters. It was the Southern Pirate's ally, the Northern Pirates!

"All men to battle!" Rick shouted. All but ten members of each ship de-boarded and started firing pistols and arrows. The rest stayed on the ship firing cannonballs and arrows at the enemy. Then Rick saw strange figures in chainmail armor. They had cone shaped hats and held small swords. They all had crosses on their chainmail, helmets and swords.

"Who are those men?" Rick asked.

"Crusaders," Cutlass said. "They spread the Proper ideology. My guess is that the Proper army needed reinforcements and sent for them."

A Crusader tried to slash Rick, but a fireball knocked him out of the sky. Heatbreath was fighting too!

"Thanks, Heatbreath!" Rick said, even though he knew Heatbreath couldn't understand his language. Rick slashed at a crusader and stabbed another. He grabbed a pistol from a Proper soldier and started to fire.

Meanwhile, another group of Crusaders were charging at a group of Northern Pirates. One of the Proper musketeers broke off from his group to help the Crusaders. He aimed at a Northern Pirate but missed. He instead, shot the lead Crusader. The other Crusaders turned to him. Immediately he dropped his musket and said, "Forget this, I'm out of here." He then jumped in the freezing water to swim away. Unfortunately, a group of white tip sharks soon ate him.

Cutlass's crew and Blackblade's crew went back onto their ships to battle at sea while the Propertorian and Northern Pirates fought on shore.

Boarded

The Elite Dark Serpent came eye to eye with Plunderer's Revenge.

"Fire the cannons!" Cutlass and Blackblade commanded at the same time. The two ships fired their cannons, severely damaging each other and killing at least 40 people. The two ships stopped, and the Elite Dark Men and Western Pirates at once boarded Plunderer's Revenge. The crew fought vigorously to defend their beloved vessel. Suddenly, there was a boom followed by another boom. Blackblade's first mate, the biggest person Rick had ever seen, stepped out of the cabin. He was about eight feet tall and had the biggest muscles ever. He looked like he could kill a whale! He boarded Cutlass's ship with ease, jumping on board with a thud. He then looked for an opponent. Crine the Cute was available. He stepped towards the baby sitting on the deck, doing nothing in the affair.

"Uh oh, someone help, I'm about to die!" Crine cried out.

"Yes, you are," the first mate said with glee. Crine was so scared he pooped in his pants.

"Eeww, can I change opponents?" The first mate asked. But then he saw Brunt and Timmy. They were shooting at Blackblade's crew. The first mate quickly snuck up behind them to kill them. Timmy turned around to see the first mate's big shadow and yelled for Brunt to look out but sadly it was too late. The first mate smashed Brunt and threw him off the deck. He was dead. A tear rolled down Timmy's face. His good pal was gone. Timmy ran away from the first mate climbing up a ladder until he was on a higher platform. The first mate went after other pirates instead of Timmy who was too high up to catch. Sadly, the first mate killed Fin and Mig too.

The Second to Last Duel

Blackblade boarded Plunderer's Revenge to fight along the next wave of Western Pirates. He landed right in front of Cutlass.

"Well, looks like we're going through the same thing we've been doing for thirty years, fighting, fighting, fighting and more fighting."

"Ye know, ye really can be a jerk sometimes, brother." Cutlass responded.

"If ye hate me so much, why do you still call me brother?"

"It would be a disgrace to the family if I didn't." Cutlass said in an angry tone.

"We're pirates! We disgrace everything. Don't tell me some of the Proper ideology has entered your noggin." Blackblade said.

"Yer the one allying with the Propers, not me." Cutlass retorted.

"I'm friends with Admiral Romeo's new wife, Alexis." Blackblade said.

"Romeo re-married?" Cutlass said astonished.

"And had a son named Alex. He is a strong believer in Proper ideology. He joined the new recruits for the Crusaders first chance he got."

"Enough with all the talking, let's just fight." Cutlass said.

Cutlass swung his axe, but Blackblade blocked without effort. He had obviously done some training in the last 14 years. Blackblade swung Ebony Blade, slashing Cutlass's chest.

"You'll pay for that brother!" Cutlass screamed. Cutlass charged at Blackblade, but the evil captain grabbed the axe from his hand.

"Let's see what happens when you can't walk," Blackblade said swinging the axe at Cutlass's leg. The Ebony Blade may have missed but the axe didn't. It hacked Cutlass's leg off. Cutlass was stunned. He couldn't fight anymore.

"Now die brother," Blackblade grunted. He kicked Cutlass off the deck into the water. He then grabbed all seven medallions from Cutlass's chamber and jumped back on board the Elite Dark Serpent, leaving Cutlass to drown.

The Saddest Sadness Any Sad Person Has Felt Since Sadness Was an Emotion

Blackblade left with the medallions. Cutlass's entire crew was sad.

"He was the best Capitano I ever had," Timmy said sobbing.

"The person who turned me from a wimpy kid into a master quick shot," Griger added.

"The only father I ever had," Rick said kneeling at the spot where Cutlass last stood.

Suddenly, to everyone's surprise, a wet Cutlass pulled himself on board the ship.

"What are you guys looking at? Get moving." He commanded.

"Great Uncle, you're alive!" Rick shouted with relief as the crew gave loud cheers.

"Nettle, get me a peg-leg. We must catch up with Blackblade without being seen."

Griger, Brakius, Dunchest, Captainsparkles, Crine the Cute, Arnold, Rick, Morano, Nettle, Timmy, Mort the Mute, Tugger, Nico, Domenden and Cutlass boarded the ship's dinghy called Tiny Skull and hurried to catch up with the Elite Dark Serpent.

Chapter 16:
Isle of the Avatorios Seas

Circle of Justice

The Elite Dark Serpent charged into the Avatorios Seas with waves crashing against it. Blackblade was determined to reach the Circle of Justice. As they approached the Circle of Justice, the crew was surprised to see it hovering over the water. Blackblade was so excited he jumped off the ship and landed on the Circle of Justice. It was a few meters in diameter, constructed from white marble which sparkled in the sunlight. It had seven slots for seven medallions. Blackblade's crew boarded a dinghy and headed to the Circle of Justice.

"In just a few minutes, we'll be more powerful than the Propers!" Blackblade exclaimed gleefully, as he placed the medallions one by one into the slots. He then jumped onto the dinghy and headed back to the Elite Dark Serpent to wait for the treasure to appear.

The Circle of Justice splashed into the water, but nothing happened. A minute went by, then **BAM!** Rising out of the water, was a humongous island full of treasure and covered by a glass dome. The dome disappeared, and heaps of gems, golden goblets, gold coins, chests and other precious items waited for the taking.

"Yes, yes, yes, yes, yes, yes, yes!!!" Blackblade laughed with delight.

"Um captain, you might want to see this." The first mate said, looking through his spy glass. "Whose ship has an insignia of a skull with two cutlasses through it?"

"It's just the remains of Cutlass's crew. Carry on runts, keep gathering the treasure, especially the golden goblet, it's mine!" Blackblade replied dismissively.

Everyone was so busy stuffing treasure into their pockets, bags and boots they didn't notice Tiny Skull had reached the Circle of Justice. Rick and the crew wasted no time on the treasure. They stormed in. Vengeance boiled in their veins.

The Portal to Die For

"Um Captain," asked the first mate, "what are we looking for?"

"The Portal to Die For," Blackblade responded. "It is in the center of the Isle of the Avatorios Sea. First mate, get ready to grab that giant treasure chest. It's the chest which holds the most prized possessions of Avatorios. And bring those chains in case we find the mystic."

"Captain, captain, I found the Portal! It was hidden under the chest!" First mate excitedly reported.

Before Blackblade could respond, he heard ***step* *tap* *step* *tap* *step* *tap*** of Captain Cutlass with his new peg-leg. The remains of the Southern Pirate Clan came into full view. They were soaked, bloody from their earlier battle and dirty from their earlier adventures. They smelled like they hadn't taken a bath in weeks! Sorry, poor choice of words. Pirates don't take baths.

"I won't let you take--," Rick could barely finish his sentence, when the Portal to Die For began bubbling and fizzing, then straight out of it came… a mystic!

The Mystic: Temal Orange Feathers

"Tie up the mystic quickly! Use these chains, we need him." Blackblade shouted at his crew.

"I am Temal Orange Feathers. You will release me under my own will!"

"I won't let you take Temal," Rick declared.

"Try and stop me!" Blackblade replied. There was no way he was going to lose the mystic, not after all the battles he had been through.

"Attack!" Cutlass shouted to his men. Rick and the others charged, attacking with all their might.

"Forget the treasure, Temal is finally ours. Keep Cutlass's crew at bay!" Blackblade commanded, as he and first mate carried Temal to the ship.

"Blackblade's getting away with Temal!" Rick yelled.

"We'll catch him. But for now, we have to fight our way out of this battle," Cutlass replied, unsure whether they would make it out alive.

final Battle

An Elite Dark Man lunged his sword at Rick. Rick dodged and knocked his opponent over. Three more were in front of Rick. One in the center slashed him, leaving a nasty gash on his chest. Rick screamed in pain. Blood dripped from the gash. Another one fired his pistol at Rick, but he dodged it narrowly and stabbed the pirate. Rick fell into a pile of gold, put two doubloons in his pocket and ran to find Cutlass, though still in pain.

Cutlass meanwhile was fighting off ten Western Pirates. Rick fired his pistols at two of them. He then jumped behind a pile of treasure and pushed it onto his opponents burying them.

"C'mon, we have to save Temal from Blackblade," Rick urged.

Rick and Cutlass ran as fast as they could towards the beach. Rick saw several pirates with Temal Orange Feather, including Blackblade. Cutlass fired his pistol at two of the pirates. Rick stabbed another two then released Temal from his chains.

"I'll get you for this," Blackblade yelled, drawing the Ebony Blade.

Suddenly, Heatbreath appeared blowing fireballs at Blackblade. The Western Pirate Captain ran for his life, barely avoiding Heatbreath's blasts. He barely managed to get on the Elite Dark Serpent before Heatbreath singed his hair off. Blackblade fired a cannonball at Heatbreath, knocking him out.

"Looks like we will have to do this without Heatbreath," Rick said.

"That's it," Cutlass said, "I know how we can stop Blackblade!"

"How?" Rick asked.

"The gunpowder barrels. If we light them on fire the Elite Dark Serpent will blow up along with the Isle of the Avatorios Seas."

"One question," Rick asked in his know-it-all voice. "How are we supposed to get close to that ship?"

"We get help. Get over here ye buffoons!" Cutlass commanded.

In seconds, the remaining crew stood in front of Cutlass looking with curious eyes.

"Alright, here's the plan. Me, Rick, and um Temal over here are gonna light the gunpowder barrels on Blackblade's ship. The rest of you are gonna cover us."

The entire crew ran towards the Elite Dark Serpent with their swords and pistols. Blackblade was on his own. He fired cannons constantly at Cutlass's crew. They quickly scattered, making it harder for Blackblade to kill them but giving enough time for Rick, Cutlass and Temal to board the Elite Dark Serpent.

The Final Confrontation

Cutlass, Rick, and Temal boarded the Elite Dark Serpent. Blackblade was still on deck dealing with the remains of Cutlass's crew who were now on the other side of the ship on a tiny dinghy. Rick set up the gunpowder barrels in the front of the ship. Temal set up the barrels in the back of the ship and Cutlass, in the middle. Rick and Temal extended the fuse cords from their barrels back to the middle barrel. If they succeeded they would be free to go their merry way. If they failed, the Western Pirate Clan would try to take over everything, including the Propers. But the Propers were much stronger and would defeat them. Then the Propers would control all of Reefia. Not the result Cutlass and his crew wanted. They had to act now.

Just as Rick was about to light the fuse, Blackblade arrived.

"Ha ha ha. I've been waiting for this moment for 14 years." Blackblade said with a loud laughter.

Rick stepped back and drew his sword, but before he could make a move, Cutlass was next to him.

"Rick," he said, "go take care of the crew."

"What do you mean?" Rick asked.

"I'll stay here and light the fuse. You get back to the dinghy."

"But you'll die. I am not leaving you."

"Ye have to. If ye don't, we will all die."

"Cutlass is right. We have to go," Temal said.

Rick felt tears roll down his cheek. He hugged Cutlass and said, "I'll never forget the captain who took me in when I was a child."

"Goodbye Rick," Cutlass said giving Rick his hat.

"Goodbye Great Uncle," Rick said. With that Temal used his magic to take Rick back to the crew.

"Ye won't live to light the fuse," Blackblade shouted. He held Ebony Blade at the ready, walked towards Cutlass, prepared to kill him.

Before Blackblade could strike, Cutlass quickly ran past him, lighting the fuse. There was a crackle as the fire split along three fuses attached to barrels of gunpowder, one in the back of the ship, another in the middle and one in the front of the ship. Blackblade tried to escape the ship by running up the stairs but Cutlass held him back, whispering into his ear, "You're going to die with me, brother!"

"Nooooooooooooooooooooooooooooooooooooooo ooo!!!!!!!!!!!!!!" Blackblade screamed.

In an instant, the ship began exploding. First, a tiny explosion happened in the middle of the ship, but then **KABOOM**, a larger explosion at the front of the ship, followed by **KABOOM**, a humongous explosion at the back of the ship. Within 30 seconds, fire engulfed the ship. To top it all off, the biggest explosion Rick had ever seen unfolded before his eyes. **KABUUUUSSSHHH!!!** Cutlass had blown himself up, taking Blackblade with him. The entire ship and Isle of the Avatorios Seas blew up.

Cutlass's crew heard Blackblade screaming as the Elite Dark Serpent sank to the bottom of the Avatorios Seas.

Disappear

Every pirate who was part of the Western Pirate Clan and all Elite Dark Men at once vanished from

Reefia. Everyone disappeared from the dock at Dark Wood. Everyone disappeared from Al-Cama. Every single Western Pirate that ever set foot on Reefia disappeared forever, leaving the Western Pirate Lands totally uninhabited.

A New Captain

"It's gone," Rick said sobbing. "We won but everything including our ship and our captain are gone. Now we are floating in a dinghy in the middle of Avatorios Seas."

"Not necessarily," Arnold said reassuringly. "We can go to several places to get a new crew. Not to mention there are more pirates still in the Southern Pirate Clan."

"We need a ship," Rick said still sobbing.

Just then, Heatbreath dropped a large treasure chest onto the dinghy. Timmy opened it to find the last ship of Avatorios, the Hydra, which he had shrunk using his magical powers and hid for all these years in the chest.

"Who is going to be Captain?" Rick asked, breathing hard, his face red as he wiped his tears.

"That's easy," Griger said, "you, of course!"

"You want me to be your captain?" Rick said astonished.

"We will follow you anywhere, Captain Rick," Timmy replied confidently.

"Count me in," Brakius said.

"Me too," Arnold said.

Soon enough the remaining crew pledged their loyalty to Captain Rick.

Rick was overcome with happiness and felt a huge responsibility. He thought for a moment. What would that mean? How can I take care of a ship? Entertain the crew? But then he knew he had to do it. He had to do it for his family and the crew.

"Tugger, you're first mate because of your loyalty to Cutlass. And Wheeler, you're going to steer the ship like you always do."

"Alright what are you waiting for Timmy," Rick said. "Drop the ship in the water and let's get out of here."

They threw the tiny ship in the water and watched as the Hydra grew to an enormous size, bigger than most pirate ships with 75 cannons on and below deck. The sails were amazingly large, and the steering wheel was just the right size for Wheeler. Now there was happiness.

Chapter 17:
Happiness

Collecting a Crew

First, they went to Pirate Island where the very first Southern Pirate crew was founded. There, Rick picked up some old geezers, including a translator for Mort the Mute.

Then they went to South Isle which had recovered from the battle 14 years ago. At South Isle, they recruited some pirate wannabees who were eager to escape the wretched Propertorian Empire.

Then they went to Antony's Outpost where they recruited at least 76 more pirates. Finally, they partied all night.

"Nice work Captain," Temal said. "You've put together quite the party."

"Oh, this crew is just the beginning," Rick replied happily. "One day we'll have a fleet big enough to take on the Propers. We will free everyone from the Propertorian Empire once and for all."

Cromund's Notes

Well, what a very epic conclusion to a very epic tale. Thank the gods Rick told me the rest of the tale years later otherwise I wouldn't be here tellin' ya. I hope you all had a lot of fun. Sorry mates, I would love to stay and chat, but I've been invited into Rick's crew. All I must say for now is:

The End

Acknowledgements

We would like to thank our parents, grandparents and siblings for their unwavering support, love and encouragement. A very big thank you to Ravi's mom for editing our story and giving us helpful suggestions along the way. Also, thanks to Lauren Berger for helping us refine the first draft of our story. Last but not least, a special thank you to Chazz Jogie for drawing the world of Reefia exactly as we imagined it. Without him we would not have a perfectly detailed map!

About the Authors

Ravi Struck is an eleven-year-old writer and fencer. He loves history, sci-fi, fantasy and graphic novels.

Josh Weisman is a twelve-year-old writer who loves fantasy, sci-fi and politics.

The two authors live in New Jersey and are best friends. They look forward to publishing more of Gromund's Tales.